For Ania

Miss Mouse's Day
A PICTURE CORGI BOOK 0552 547441

First published in Great Britain by Doubleday,
an imprint of Random House Children's Books

Doubleday edition published 2001
Picture Corgi edition published 2002

1 3 5 7 9 10 8 6 4 2

Picture Corgi Books are published by Random House Children's Books,
61-63 Uxbridge Road, London W5 5SA,
a division of The Random House Group Ltd,
in Australia by Random House Australia (Pty) Ltd,
20 Alfred Street, Milsons Point, Sydney, NSW 2061, Australia,
in New Zealand by Random House New Zealand Ltd,
18 Poland Road, Glenfield, Auckland 10, New Zealand,
and in South Africa by Random House (Pty) Ltd,
Endulini, 5A Jubilee Road, Parktown 2193, South Africa

THE RANDOM HOUSE GROUP Limited Reg. No. 954009
www.booksattransworld.co.uk/childrens

A CIP catalogue record for this book is available from the British Library.

Miss Mouse's Day

Miss Mouse's Day

That's me!

by Jan Ormerod

Picture Corgi

MY DAY BY ME, MISS MOUSE,

starts with a cuddle,

then a story.

Then I get dressed.

Too hot!

Too big!

Too frilly!

Just right.

For breakfast I like

strawberries

and eggs

and orange juice

and jam.

Time to wash up.

Then I like to draw.

I use pencils

and crayons,

watercolours

and finger paints.

I can't see. . . .   WOW! It's me!

Dressing up is fun.

Too fancy.

Too spooky.

Too scary.

I like lipstick best . . .

and stars, and stripy socks.

I'm gorgeous!

A little lunch.

Then a little exercise.

Whee!   Oops.   HELP!

Saved!

I'm a very fine slider . . .

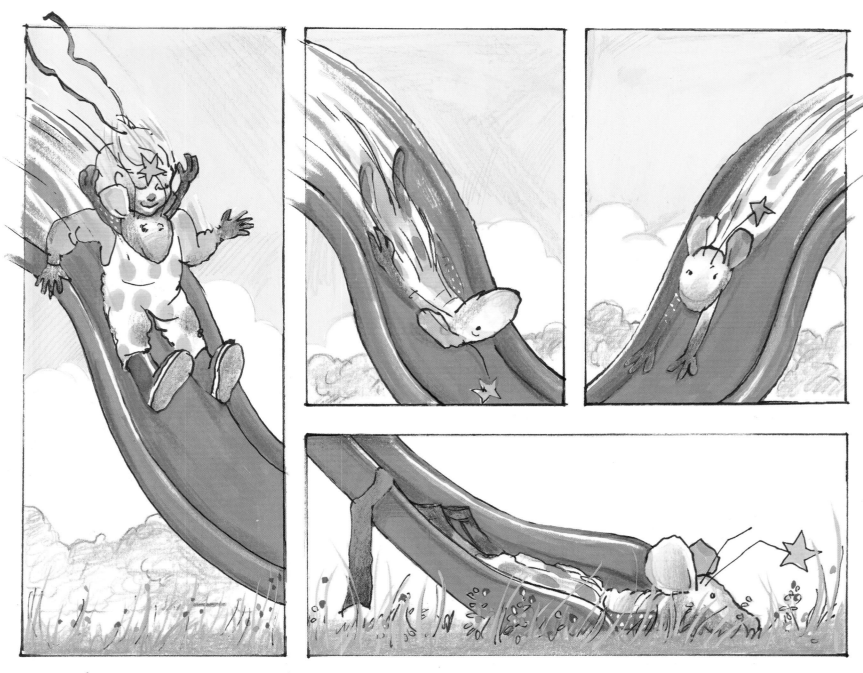

mostly.

I'm a super builder.

Push,

pull,

dig.

A house!

Two houses.   Three houses.

A whole city!

I love flowers  and mud.

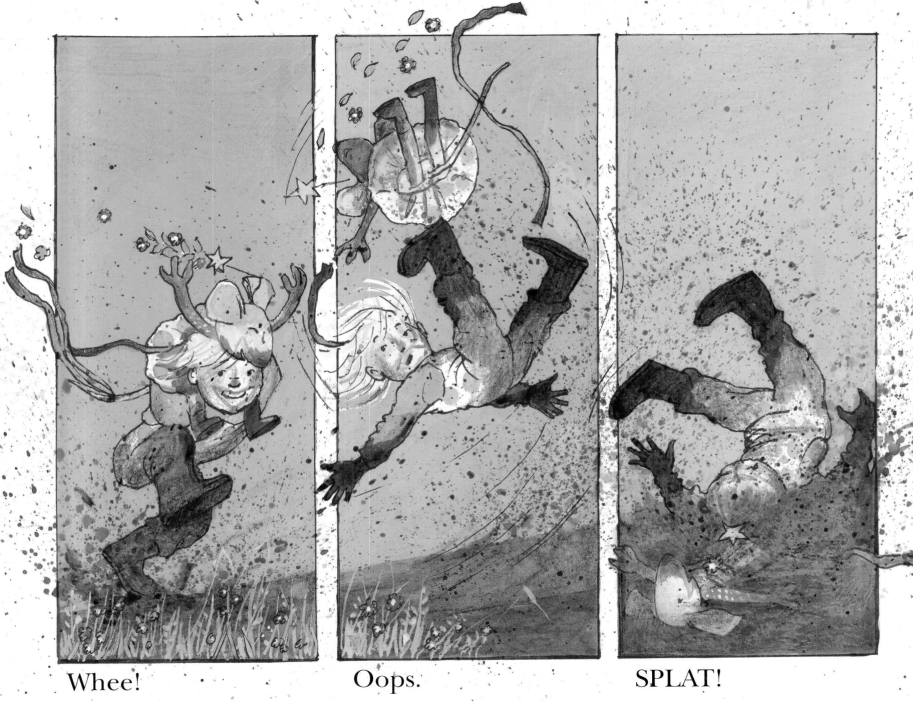

Whee!   Oops.   SPLAT!

"What a mess!

To the bath!"

Oh, dear.   Don't forget me!   Uh-oh . . .

Is that a light?   Whew!

Wash,

wring,

towel,

spin:

clean and dry.

Quiet games

and a story.　　A yawn,　　then off to bed.

A good night kiss, and my day ends . . .

with a cuddle.

Good night!